STAR WARS®

THE FORCE AWAKENS

Read-Along
STORYBOOK AND CD

A long time ago in a galaxy far, far away, there was a scavenger, a soldier, and a lost droid. This is the story of *Star Wars: The Force Awakens*. You can read along with me in your book. You'll know it's time to turn the page when you hear this sound. . . .

Let's begin now.

Printed in the United States of America

First Edition, April 2016   10 9 8 7 6 5 4 3 2 1

Library of Congress Number on file

FAC-008598-16060

ISBN 978-1-4847-3149-9

DISNEP
LUCASFILM
PRESS

Los Angeles • New York

SUSTAINABLE FORESTRY INITIATIVE — Certified Chain of Custody — At Least 20% Certified Forest Content — www.sfiprogram.org — SFI-00993

For Text Only

POE DAMERON WAS ON A MISSION. The Resistance had sent the pilot and his trusty droid, BB-8, to recover a map that would help the group find Luke Skywalker. Luke was a powerful Jedi Knight, known for defeating the evil Empire. But Luke had disappeared many years before. A new enemy, the First Order, threatened to destroy peace in the galaxy, and the Resistance needed Luke once more.

Poe and BB-8's mission took them to a small village on the sandy planet of Jakku. There, Lor San Tekka—an old friend of Luke's—gave the map to Poe.

But moments later, First Order stormtroopers attacked the village.

"On my command! Fire!"

Poe and BB-8 fled to their ship, but it was quickly destroyed by the stormtroopers. Poe knew he had to get the map to safety. He gave it to BB-8 and ran back to help Lor.

But someone else had reached the old man first. Kylo Ren, a vicious warrior for the First Order, held Lor captive.

"You know what I've come for."

Poe fired at Kylo, but it was no use. Kylo used the Force to deflect Poe's blasts and quickly captured the Resistance pilot.

Kylo, Poe, and the stormtroopers returned to the First Order Star Destroyer orbiting Jakku. The soldiers went back to their barracks—all except one stormtrooper named FN-2187. That battle had been his first, and he hoped it would be his last. He felt terrible about the attack and had only pretended to fire his blaster at the villagers on Jakku.

Suddenly, the stormtrooper heard a voice behind him.

"FN-2187. Submit your blaster for inspection."

It was his commanding officer, Captain Phasma. She suspected that FN-2187 had failed to fire on anyone in the village, but she wanted to prove it.

FN-2187 was ready to leave the First Order, but he'd need a pilot to help him escape. Fortunately, he knew just where to find one. . . .

Meanwhile, on Jakku, a scavenger named Rey was searching through a crashed starship for spare parts. She was looking for anything she could use or trade for food nearby at Niima Outpost.

It was a hard life, but it was the only one Rey had ever known.

All that changed, however, when she came across a little round droid. The droid was lost and refused to leave her side.

On board the Star Destroyer, FN-2187 had freed Poe, but they still needed to get off the ship.

The trooper asked the pilot if he could fly a Special Forces TIE fighter.

"I can fly anything."

Together, FN-2187 and Poe stole one of the enemy ships and escaped into space.

"I always wanted to fly one of these things. I'm Poe. Poe Dameron."

Poe asked if he could call the soldier Finn instead, and the former stormtrooper happily agreed.

Poe told Finn that they needed to head back to Jakku and find his droid, BB-8. But Finn protested.

"We go back to Jakku, we die."

But there was no time to argue. A blast from the Star Destroyer suddenly rocked their ship.

Poe looked over at Finn in the gunner's seat.

"Now would be a good time to start shootin'."

But it was too late. Alarms rang as their TIE fighter plummeted toward the sandy planet below.

Finn managed to eject before the ship hit the ground. But the only sign of Poe was his jacket. Finn grabbed the jacket and shed his stormtrooper armor before heading across the hot desert. He needed to find help.

After wandering for hours, Finn finally found an outpost. He was shocked when he saw the droid Poe had described.

BB-8 was still at Rey's side. Finn did his best to tell Rey everything about BB-8's mission for the Resistance, but it was a complicated story.

"Listen, I've had a pretty messed-up day."

And the day was about to get worse. A team of stormtroopers was searching the outpost for the lost droid.

Finn, Rey, and BB-8 looked for somewhere to hide, but the stormtroopers had already spotted them.

Rey knew they couldn't escape the stormtroopers on foot. But they might be able to in a ship! She led them toward the shipyard, and they hopped aboard an old Corellian light freighter that hadn't been flown in years. Rey fired up the engines and took off while Finn hurried to the gunner's seat.

Two TIE fighters flew down and fired on them! Finn took aim and fired back.

Rey heard his blaster bolts strike a direct hit.

"Nice shot!"

But Finn saw that the TIE fighters were still close behind them.
"We need cover!"

Rey banked hard and turned the ship toward the fields of wreckage out in the desert. Finn shot down one of the TIEs. Then Rey flew right through the inside of a crashed Star Destroyer, catching the other TIE off guard. Finn fired and the enemy ship exploded in a shower of sparks.

Rey quickly flew into space, breathing a sigh of relief.

Now they could get BB-8 and the map back to the Resistance. But even though they had escaped the First Order, there were other dangers lurking.

As Rey and Finn were planning what to do next, their ship suddenly lost power.

"Someone's locked on to us. All controls have been overridden!"

A massive cargo hauler loomed above their ship, pulling them into its docking bay.

Finn, Rey, and BB-8 hid, listening as two strangers boarded the ship. The newcomers immediately began looking through the ship and within moments found the trio's hiding place. To Finn and Rey's surprise, the two figures were an old man and a Wookiee.

"Chewie, we're home."

The man introduced himself as Han Solo and explained that the ship—the *Millennium Falcon*—was his.

Rey recognized his name at once. Han was one of the heroes who had helped Luke Skywalker defeat the Empire.

Since that time, Han and Chewbacca had been involved in some decidedly less heroic jobs. Even as Han was talking to Rey and Finn, two rival gangs boarded the cargo ship and demanded payment for one of Han's failed missions. Han, Chewie, and their three new friends escaped to the *Millennium Falcon* and jumped to lightspeed.

"Hang on back there."

Safe again for the moment, Rey explained that BB-8 had a map that would help lead the Resistance to Luke Skywalker.

"This droid has to get to the Resistance base as soon as possible."

Then BB-8 projected the map he had been protecting.

Upon hearing the name of his old friend, Han agreed to help.

Han thought his friend Maz might be able to help, too. They flew to the lush planet of Takodana, where Maz's castle provided refuge for every human and alien in that corner of the galaxy.

Maz sized each of them up, finally turning to Rey. The short alien asked about Rey's past and gazed up at her with big questioning eyes.

Rey shifted uncomfortably.

"I'm no one. I'm just a scavenger."

Maz disagreed. She suggested that Rey was in tune with the Force, but the girl didn't believe her. Rey fled the castle. She wanted to find somewhere she could be alone.

But even Maz's castle wasn't safe from the First Order. A spy among Maz's guests had called down troops to attack.

Han, Chewie, and Finn did their best to fight off the First Order stormtroopers.

Maz had given Finn a lightsaber, which he used to clear his way through the battle.

He had to find Rey!

It was too late, though. Kylo Ren had found Rey first. She fired at him, but her blaster was no match for Kylo's lightsaber. Kylo captured her and took her back to his shuttle.

Han, Finn, and the others were able to escape only after a squad of Resistance ships appeared in the sky. They had finally been able to track down BB-8's homing signal and had arrived to help!

The Resistance forces, led by General Leia Organa, escorted the *Millennium Falcon* safely back to their base.

Once there, Finn was surprised to see a familiar face: Poe Dameron's! The pilot had survived the crash on Jakku and was once again flying for the Resistance.

BB-8 beeped with joy as he reunited with Poe.

The Resistance had learned that the First Order completed work on a massive weapon called the Starkiller that could destroy entire star systems. The First Order had already used the planet-sized weapon to obliterate the New Republic capital. The Resistance was the only force left to stop the evil group.

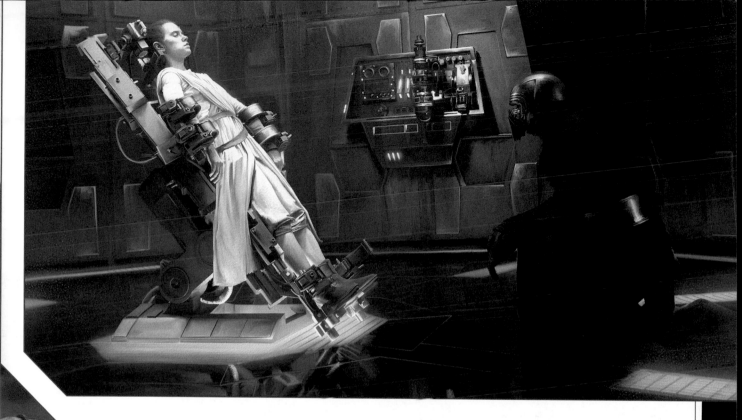

After the battle of Takodana, Kylo took Rey to the frozen planet that housed the Starkiller. There he questioned her, trying to learn any information she might be hiding.

"Is it true? You're just a scavenger?"

Rey was surprised to hear the echo of her own words in Kylo's question. As she looked into the villain's eyes, she sensed a connection between them. It was almost as if she could see into his mind. . . .

Suddenly, Rey was flooded with images and emotions. She could see Kylo's anger and hurt . . . and fear. Kylo pulled back. He couldn't believe it. Was she using the Force? One thing was clear: Rey was more than just a scavenger.

Meanwhile, the Resistance was planning its attack on the Starkiller base. Han, Chewie, and Finn would land on the enemy base and take down its shields from the inside. Then Poe and his team of pilots could fly in and destroy the crucial part of the weapon that kept it from overheating. The Starkiller would explode in a massive power overload.

Finn also hoped he could find Rey and rescue her from Kylo Ren. Poe wished Finn luck, then hopped into his X-wing and took off.

"All teams, altitude confirmed, hold for jump to lightspeed on my go."

Alone in her cell, Rey was still recovering from the strange experience
of looking into Kylo's mind. She felt different and powerful. She wondered if
she could do it again. . . .

Rey called to the guard in her cell and ordered him to remove her
restraints. To her surprise, he did. Rey ran from the cell and quietly scaled
the walls of the base, searching for a way to escape.

Han, Chewie, and Finn had just landed on the Starkiller base.
They could see a great beam extending into the sky, drawing in power from a nearby star. Once the star was extinguished, the weapon would be ready to fire. They had to destroy the Starkiller before that happened.

They fought their way deep into the Starkiller base. First Order forces were everywhere and time was running out! Finn spotted Captain Phasma. His old commander would know exactly how to get to the shields!

Chewie grabbed the unsuspecting captain. When Phasma saw Finn, she tried to call him by his old identification code.

Finn corrected her.

"The name's Finn. And I'm in charge now."

Phasma had no choice. She led them to the shields' controls and disabled them.

Poe and his pilots circled high above the Starkiller base.

"Red Squad, Blue Squad, take my lead."

The First Order's fleet was firing at them. Poe dodged blast after blast, taking his squad around for another attack run.

Then he received the message he had been waiting for: the Starkiller's shields were down!

Poe smiled.

"Alright, let's light it up!"

But as the X-wings fired, the Resistance pilots discovered that there was still a dense wall between them and the weapon's cooling device.

From the Starkiller base, Finn saw the X-wings attacking. He realized they had to take the wall down. But as soon as they did, it would be only a matter of time until the base exploded.

Fortunately, Rey ran right into them!

Together, Han, Chewie, Finn, and Rey sprinted toward the cooling device.

Han and Chewie planted explosives while Rey and Finn kept watch for stormtroopers. But it wasn't stormtroopers who found them. It was Kylo Ren! He was searching the area for Resistance forces when Han saw him approaching. Instead of raising his blaster, Han stepped out of the shadows and called out to Kylo.

Kylo spun around and looked at Han.

"I've been waiting for this day for a long time."

So had Han. Ever since Kylo had fallen to the dark side of the Force, Han had been waiting for his son to return to him. Now the Starkiller was about to be destroyed, and Han reached out to Kylo one last time, begging him to come home.

But Kylo would not listen. He ignited his lightsaber and silenced his father forever.

Chewie cried out in horror. But he still had a mission to complete. He managed to set off the explosives, but a squad of stormtroopers separated him from Finn and Rey.

Finn and Rey ran through the twisting hallways of the Starkiller base. They felt the planet rock beneath their feet as Poe fired on the weakened cooling device, destroying it once and for all. Now they just had to get back to their ship!

But when they reached the edge of the base, Kylo Ren was waiting for them. Finn drew the lightsaber Maz had given him.

Kylo sneered.

"That weapon . . . is mine."

"Come get it."

Finn used every ounce of his training to fight Kylo, but it wasn't enough. Only someone with a strong connection to the Force could defeat such a warrior. With a mighty blow, Kylo knocked Finn to the ground, wounding him.

Kylo used the Force to pull Finn's lightsaber from his grip. The weapon flew toward Kylo . . . and then sped right past him and into Rey's waiting hand! She ignited the weapon and charged at Kylo.

Rey's blue lightsaber clashed against the burning red of Kylo's. Anger filled her as she struck blow after blow against the man who had hurt her friends. She could feel the Force within her, surging with power.

Kylo hit the ground as Rey's lightsaber cut across his face. Rey realized she could end everything. She could destroy Kylo for good.

Suddenly, the Starkiller base rumbled beneath their feet. A great gulf opened between them as the planet began to tear itself apart. Kylo was beyond her reach, but she had defeated him for now.

Rey knelt beside Finn as stormtroopers arrived and helped the injured Kylo to a shuttle.

Chewie picked up Rey and Finn in the *Falcon*. Rey took the pilot's seat at the Wookiee's side, and together they set course for the Resistance base. Behind them, the planet collapsed in a burst of light and heat. The Resistance had destroyed the weapon once and for all!

Back at the Resistance base, Rey still had a long journey ahead of her. The First Order had been crippled but not defeated. Kylo and his soldiers would return.

The Resistance knew that Rey needed to be taught the ways of the Force and that only Luke Skywalker could train her.

Carrying BB-8's precious map and the lightsaber Maz had given Finn, Rey said good-bye to Leia and boarded the *Millennium Falcon* alongside Chewbacca and R2-D2.

They were off to find the lost Jedi.

When the *Millennium Falcon* reached Ahch-To, an old man was waiting for Rey. Luke Skywalker was strong in the Force and had sensed her arrival.

Rey handed the Jedi Master the lightsaber. It was his, after all.

Rey didn't know what the future held. But she was sure that her adventures were only just beginning. . . .